SOPHIE and LOU

Petra Mathers

DANCE-FEVER

HarperTrophy

A Division of HarperCollinsPublishers

Sophie and Lou
Copyright © 1991 by Petra Mathers
Printed in the U.S.A. All rights reserved.

Library of Congress Cataloging-in-Publication Data
Mathers, Petra.
    Sophie and Lou / by Petra Mathers.
        p.   cm.
    Summary: Shy Sophie, enticed by the dancing that she sees in the
studio across the street, sets out to learn on her own.
    ISBN 0-06-024071-7. — ISBN 0-06-024072-5 (lib. bdg.)
    ISBN 0-06-443331-5 (pbk.)
    [1.Dancing—Fiction.]   I. Title.
PZ7.M42475So   1991   90-37562
[E]—dc20   CIP
                                                                   AC

Typography by Christine Kettner
First Harper Trophy edition, 1993.

To Love

and those who dare put all their eggs in one basket

Sophie was shy—so shy she did her shopping during the lull hours, so she wouldn't have to talk to anyone.

Every Wednesday the Book-Mobile parked in front of the supermarket, and every Wednesday Sophie *almost* went in. But the librarian was so tall!

Sophie walked home minding her bags and watching her feet.

Sophie's house was dust free. The furniture gleamed, the windows shone. She could sit for a long time watching the sun creep across the walls.

One morning she heard pounding and shouting across the street.

"Oh, my," she said, twirling her duster, "what are they up to over there? Nobody's been in that house for years."

During the following weeks, Sophie watched anxiously as the building was torn apart and put back together again. A banner went up: KICK UP YOUR HEELS, Dolores and Rudi, Dance Studio.

"Lots of strangers coming and going," she said. One of the strangers tipped his hat. Sophie drew the curtains.

Dolores and Rudi danced well together. Little snatches of music came in waves. Sophie saw a few students now and then.

They brought friends, and the friends brought friends.

Soon Sophie couldn't stay away from her window.

"Gentlemen, gentlemen," Rudi would cry, clapping, "LEAD your lady, don't push her. Elbows up, please, nose over the toes, and again, one, two, three, four."

"Ladies, ladies," Dolores would plead, "straight backs, but move those legs. Glide, don't march. LOOK at your partner, then s l o w l y up at the chandelier and down to the right.

"And now again, one, two, look-at-your-partner-three, four, and WHAT-A-BEAUTIFUL-CHANDELIER-three, four..."

"What are they doing with their *feet*?" Sophie wondered before she fell asleep.

On Wednesday she climbed the stairs to the Book-Mobile.

"Do you"—she swallowed—"do you have any books on learning how to dance?"

"Certainly," said the tall librarian, and knew just where to reach.

Sophie took her books and fled.

Safe at home again, Sophie pushed all the furniture against the walls and painted dancing steps on the floor.

Blue for waltz, red for tango, green for fox-trot, orange for polka, and purple for samba.

She practiced during the day, humming and counting. At night she danced along with Dolores and Rudi. When they stopped, she stopped. When they started again, so did she.

She watched herself in the mirror.

"I look mousy," she decided one night. "I need something that swings and bounces."

She looked into her closet. "Who wants to come out and dance?" she called. Way in the back hung her old best, but the shoes were hopeless.

The next day, hiding behind her shopping bags, Sophie slipped into a shoe store. "I need some shoes, please," she whispered. "I'm a dancer," she added a little louder, and sat down.

There were boxes and boxes full of shoes. She tried them all.

"Where do you dance?" the saleslady asked.

"Oh, with Dolores and Rudi," Sophie said, blushing.

On her way out, someone rushed to open the door for her. Sophie knew she had seen him before. I like his face, she thought.

All the way home, she danced inside.

That night Sophie put on her old best, and new shoes. Finally, she heard Dolores. "Your positions, ladies. Pick your partners."

"Oh, well, here we go all alone, one, two, three, four," Sophie sang, barely looking at the green steps for fox-trot. She circled and swayed, all the while holding her arms out to the empty air around her.

"And now, ladies, look-at-your-partner-three, four, and oh-what-a...*STOP, STOP, STOP.*"

The music stopped, but Sophie went on, "...beautiful-chandelier-three, four, because-she-knew-she-had-it-three, four..."

The doorbell rang.

"...and-to-the-door-three, four, and-open-wide-three..."

"My name is Lou," he said, bowing from the waist. "May I have this dance?"

"You bet," said Sophie, and stepped into his arms.